I0601125

The Swine of Avon

by Thomas Hischak

A SAMUEL FRENCH ACTING EDITION

FOUNDED 1830

SAMUELFRENCH.COM

CHARACTERS

12-24 actors, each character can be played by a male or female

Pigskin and **Pigsty,** two tour guides
Shankspeare, the greatest playwright of all Swinedom
Mama, Shankspeare's mother
Boarbage, a famous actor and manager of the Glob Playhouse
Swill Kemp, a comic actor
Good Queen BLT the First, reigning monarch of Swinedom
Sir Frankfurt Bacon, a scientist and scholar
A Spy, Stranger, Publisher, piglets, tourists, actors, theatregoers,
    and **students**

Also these characters from Shankspeare's plays, performed by the
actors who portray the above characters:

Don Armadillo, a Spanish nobleman
Mouth, a youth
King Porkrind the Third, a villainous swine
Porkchopio, an Italian ruffian
Katerina Pigiron, a shrew
Porkeron, king of the fairies
Canadian Bacon, queen of the fairies
Pickled-Pig's-Feet, a mischievous spirit
Hogwild, a union foreman
Peter Curlytail, a union worker
Julius Razorback, a Roman general
Brute Chops, a Roman nobleman
MacBoar, thane of Scotland
Lady MacBoar, his wife
Hamhock, Prince of Denmark
Burptrude, Queen of Denmark
Baloneyus, a courtier
Swineo and Drooliet, two young lovers
Porcino, a wizard

PRODUCTION NOTES

The comedy is performed by a company of pigs and any character can be played by a male or female actor. Doubling is possible and the commentary by Pigskin and Pigsty can be delivered by the other actors if one wishes to eliminate those roles.

The play is meant to be performed on an open stage with only props and a few furniture pieces. Each of the actors wears a simple pig nose on an elastic string. The rest of the costume can be simple modern clothes with perhaps a hat, rehearsal skirt or Elizabethan collar used on occasion to indicate a specific character.

This play may be presented with Thomas Hischak's one-act Shakespeare-related comedy CURST BE HE WHO MOVES MY BONES for a full evening of theare titled DOUBLE BARD TROUBLE.

SUGGESTED DOUBLING FOR A CAST OF TWELVE ACTORS

Actor 1 — Shankspeare

Actor 2 — Boarbage/Don Armadillo/Porkrind III

Actor 3 — Mama/Queen BLT/Lady MacBoar

Actor 4 — Swill Kemp/Porkeron/MacBoar

Actor 5 — Sir Frankfurt Bacon/Pickled-Pig's Feet/Hamhock

Actor 6 — Publisher/Canadian Bacon/Drooliet/Student 2

Actor 7 — Porkchopio/Brute Chop/Porcino

Actor 8 — Mouth/Katerina Pigiron/ Burptrude

Actor 9 — Spy/Peter Curlytail/Baloneyus/Student 1

Actor 10 — Stranger/Hogwild/Swineo/Julius Razorback

Actor 11 — Pigskin

Actor 12 — Pigsty

(PIGSKIN ENTERS, stops and turns, calling offstage.)

PIGSKIN. Right this way, ladies and gentlemen! This way, please!

(Half of the company ENTERS as TOURISTS and join PIGSKIN. They wear loud shirts, straw hats and several carry cameras.)

TOURISTS. Oink! Oink! Oink! Oink! Oink!

PIGSKIN. We are now at one of the most famous of all landmarks here in the town of Fatsford-on-Avon. *(Points out toward audience.)* Here is the birthplace of the great author, Shankspeare.

TOURISTS. Oink! Oink! Oink! Oink! Oink! *(Some take pictures.)*

PIGSKIN. It was in this humble little pigpen that Shankspeare was born. The pen has been restored by the historical society so that it looks exactly as it did in Shankspeare's day. Notice how even the straw and the slop are very authentic.

TOURISTS. *(Impressed)* Oink! Oink!

PIGSKIN. It was in this pigpen that Shankspeare was given a basic education by the mother pig and other sows. It was first here that the young Shankspeare learned snorting, grunting, slobbering, French, iambic pentameter, and Pig Latin. You are-ooking-lay at the-ipgsty-pay of a-enius-jay!

TOURISTS. *(Even more impressed; more pictures are taken.)* Oink! Oink!

PIGSKIN. You may enter the pigpen to get a closer look. But, please, do not touch anything.

(PIGSKIN and the TOURISTS freeze in position. From the opposite side of the stage, PIGSTY ENTERS, turns, and calls offstage. The sounds of modern car and truck traffic are heard.)

PIGSTY. Come this way, ladies and gentlemen! Please stay on the sidewalk. The traffic is rather heavy. This way!

(The other half of the company ENTERS as TOURISTS and joins PIGSTY. They are dressed in a similar manner and also have cameras.)

TOURISTS. Snort! Snort! Snort! Snort! Snort!

PIGSTY. That's right…stay on the curb. Very good. At this rather busy intersection lies one of the greatest landmarks in the whole city of Loin-don: the site of the original Glob Theatre.

TOURISTS. Snort! Snort! Snort! Snort! Snort! *(Some take pictures.)*

PIGSTY. On this corner stood the playhouse that has forever been associated with the name of Shankspeare, the greatest playwright of all Swinedom. It was here that such beloved plays as *All's Sow That Ends Sow, Corioloinus, The Merry Warthogs of Windsor, Much Ado About Hogwash,* and *Two Gentle-Hams of Verona* were first performed.

TOURISTS. *(Impressed)* Snort! Snort!

PIGSTY. Shankspeare is believed to have acted at the Glob Playhouse, though mostly in smaller roles. As a writer Shankspeare was a masterful artist; but as an actor, it is believed the pig was something of a ham. *(TOURISTS laugh.)* Just my little joke. Now if you all would turn left . . .

(PIGPEN and the first group of tourists unfreeze.)

PIGSKIN. Are there any questions? I would be happy to answer them. *(One pig raises her hand.)*

PIGSTY. At this time I will entertain any questions you might have. *(A second pig raises his hand.)*

PIGSKIN. Yes, madam?

TOURIST FROM FIRST GROUP. Oink oink oink oink oink oink oink oink oink?

PIGSTY. You there? You have a question?

TOURIST FROM SECOND GROUP. Snort snort snort snort snort snort snort snort?

PIGSKIN. A very good question, madam, and one which scholars have endeavored to answer for over four hundred years.

PIGSTY. An interesting question and one well worth asking.

PIGSKIN. How did such a humble, small-town pig like Shankspeare rise to become the most famous literary giant of all Swinedom?

PIGSTY. How was it possible for one single, mortal swine to possess so much knowledge and creativity?

PIGSKIN. In order to attempt to determine the answer, we must go back and examine the life of this extraordinary pig...

PIGSTY. To understand how such a thing was possible, one must look carefully at all the facts and try to recreate the situation...

(PIGSKIN and PIGSTY move downstage and continue, addressing the audience, as the TOURISTS EXIT left and right.)

PIGSKIN. It is 1564 and, in the village of Fatsford-on-Avon, Shankspeare is born into a large family...

PIGSTY. The middle child of sixteen brothers and sisters and the runt of a liter of five piglets born one April day.

PIGSKIN. But from the very beginning Shankspeare was different from the rest...

PIGSTY. Discontented, dreamy, restless, anxious, moody...

PIGSKIN. Not your usual pig in a poke.

(MAMA ENTERS and calls to her piglets off stage.)

MAMA. Sooooo-eeee!

(SHANKSPEARE and the PIGLETS ENTER. They line up behind MAMA and SHANKSPEARE and, with their backs to the audience, hunch over an imaginary feeding trough and eat noisily.)

PIGLETS. Snort Snort! Grunt Grunt! Slobber! Slobber! Snort Snort! Grunt Grunt! Slobber! Slobber!

MAMA. Shankspeare, why aren't you eating with your brothers and sisters?

SHANKSPEARE. I'm not hungry, Mama.

MAMA. Not hungry? Ridiculous! Since when do you have to be hungry to make a pig of yourself. Go! Eat!

SHANKSPEARE. Is that all life is, Mama? Eating and snorting and grunting?

PIGLETS. Slobber slobber slobber!

SHANKSPEARE. And slobbering?

MAMA. Oh, my poor dear Shankspeare! Asking such questions! How I worry about you!

SHANKSPEARE. It seems that there is more to our existence than what I see here in Fatsford. What about the rest of the world?

MAMA. I don't know what the rest of the world is like, my dearest. I've never traveled anywhere. You could ask your father. He was once taken to a county fair in Burgerham. He won a prize of some sort.

SHANKSPEARE. For being a hog. What kind of prize is that?

MAMA. Well, he couldn't very well win it for being a swan! Now, try eating a little something.

SHANKSPEARE. I feel I am destined to do more with my life. Something that will glorify myself and all of my kind. What a piece of work is a pig, how noble in reason! How infinite in faculty!

MAMA. Don't be such a boar, dear. Save the fancy talk for later. Now go and get your snout into that trough like a good little piglet.

SHANKSPEARE. Yes, Mama…

MAMA. Then later the whole family will have a belching contest. Won't that be fun?

SHANKSPEARE. I suppose so…*(Turns and joins PIGLETS.)*

MAMA. What's to become of that little porker, I don't know. I'm afraid it's just another case of pearls before swine.

(MAMA, SHANKSPEARE and the PIGLETS sit downstage with their backs to the audience as the ACTORS ENTER and take their positions on a temporary stage.)

PIGSKIN. Shankspeare might have lived forever the life of a discontented swine in a backwater town…

PIGSTY. But something happened one day that changed the direction of the young pig's life.

PIGSKIN. A troupe of strolling actors, called the Porkrind Players, set up a simple stage in the market square of Fatsford-on-Avon, and performed a play.

(The ACTORS act out the play in dumbshow with plenty of exaggerated gestures and a lot of swinging of wooden swords.)

PIGSTY. They were not the most accomplished of performers and the little drama was rather crude...

ACTOR 1. "Unhand that maiden, sirrah, or I'll puncture your porcine paunch with this prickly pear of a poker!"

ACTOR 2. "Are you addressing me, sausageface?"

ACTOR 1. "Yea! Release Miss Piggy or, prithee, you'll pay the price that every pigheaded porker pays who purloins pure princesses such as she!"

PIGSKIN. Poetry in the theatre was somewhat at a low point...

PIGSTY. But it didn't matter. Shankspeare was mesmerized by the theatrical event and inspiration filled the young pig's heart.

(SHANKSPEARE rises and turns toward the audience. All the others, but PIGPEN and PIGSTY, EXIT.)

SHANKSPEARE. Now my life has a purpose! I will join the theatrical profession and bring drama and romance to audiences everywhere!

PIGSKIN. Some say that Shankspeare left Fatsford that very day, stealing out of the pig pen late at night and joining the players as they rode out of town in their hog cart.

SHANKSPEARE. Goodbye, Fatsford-on-Avon! Farewell familiar old pig pen. It's an actor's life for me! *(EXITS)*

PIGSTY. There is no record of Shankspeare in Fatsford after 1585 and seven years later the name shows up as an actor in the capitol city of Loin-don.

PIGSKIN. Those unaccounted-for seven years remain a mystery that has puzzled and intrigued scholars for centuries.

PIGSTY. Where was Shankspeare during that time and what was the pig doing?

PIGSKIN. Perhaps Shankspeare was a traveling actor but there is no proof.

PIGSTY. Some believe that the future-poet joined the army and saw combat in France.

(SHANKSPEARE ENTERS wearing a helmet and swinging a sword.)

SHANKSPEARE. Once more unto the breech…! *(Rushes across the stage then stops suddenly.)* There's a hell of a lot of French pigs over there. And they all have swords! *(Starts backing up.)* They're coming this way! *(Runs in opposite direction.)* Stand not on the order of your going but…run wee wee wee wee all the way home!! *(EXITS)*

PIGSKIN. Some have argued that Shankspeare became a teacher during this period and taught Latin to private pupils.

(SHANKSPEARE ENTERS carrying a stack of books, followed by two STUDENT pigs.)

SHANKSPEARE. Today we are going to study the orations of Cicero.

STUDENT 1. I hate Cicero. When do we eat?

SHANKSPEARE. Then we will look at the poetry of Virgil.

STUDENT 2. Virgil! Yeeuch! I'm hungry!

STUDENT 1. Me too! Let's eat!

BOTH. Snort! Snort! Snort!

SHANKSPEARE. Listen to me, you suckling pigs. I'm talking about a whole new kind of nourishment: the food of knowledge!

BOTH. Huh?

SHANKSPEARE. Not food for the body but food for the soul. The majesty of words, the beauty of ideas, the glory of poetry!

STUDENT 2. I'd rather have swill!

STUDENT 1. Me too!

BOTH. Oink oink oink oink oink!

SHANKSPEARE. Let me teach you the dialogues of Plato, the ideas of Erasmus, the philosophy of Bacon—!

BOTH. Bacon? Ahhhhhh! *(They run off frightened.)*

SHANKSPEARE. A little learning is a dangerous thing. I wonder who said that. *(EXITS)*

PIGSTY. One theory has it that Shankspeare went to sea as a sailor during this mysterious period.

(SHANKSPEARE ENTERS wearing a sailor cap.)

SHANKSPEARE. Ah! The bracing sea air, the crash of the waves, the spewing of the foam, the screaming of the gulls, the rocking and rolling of the deck…*(Starts to feel seasick.)* The constant rocking…The continuous rolling…The endless, insistent, merciless rocking and rolling— ! *(Runs offstage sick.)*

PIGSKIN. There is even a theory that during those unaccounted-for seven years Shankspeare was a spy for the government of Swinedom.

(SHANKSPEARE, wearing a conspicuous long cloak with a hood, ENTERS with a pig SPY who carries a letter.)

SPY. After you read the contents of this letter, you must memorize what it says and not divulge the information under any circumstances.

SHANKSPEARE. Certainly.

SPY. Even if you are captured and tortured, you must not utter one word of what is written here.

SHANKSPEARE. Tortured?

SPY. Even if they tear out your tongue and burn your hoofs off, you must remain loyal to the Queen.

SHANKSPEARE. I promise. If they tear out my tongue, I won't say a word.

SPY. Good. Read the letter. *(Hands SHANKSPEARE the letter.)*

SHANKSPEARE. *(Reads aloud.)* "The map to the money for the military is under the molehill in the mire one mile from the mulch mill on the moorings of the Moloch River in Middleton."

SPY. Exactly. Memorize it, eat the letter, then off you go.

SHANKSPEARE. Memorize, eat, then go. Got it.

SPY. God save the Queen!

SHANKSPEARE. God save the Queen! *(SPY EXITS; reads the letter again.)* "The map to the money for the military is under the molehill in the mire one mile from the mulch mill on the moorings of the Moloch River in Middleton." That's easy. *(Folds letter.)* "The map to the money for the molehill is in the mulch —" That's not right. *(Looks at letter again.)* "…under the molehill in the mire one mile…the Moloch River in Middleton…" I've got it. *(Folds letter.)* "The map to the military mulch is moldy in Maryland but moored in Manila—"

(A suspicious pig STRANGER also in a cloak ENTERS and sees SHANKSPEARE.)

STRANGER. Who goes there?

SHANKSPEARE. Huh? Oh! *(Shoves the letter into his mouth and chews.)* The mmmm mooo munnn maaaa mmmmm muuu morrrr…

STRANGER. Doesn't speak our language. Maybe it's a spy.

SHANKSPEARE. Mo! *(Shakes head.)* Meeee mooooo

mnnnnnn! *(Starts to EXIT.)*

STRANGER. More like the village idiot. Move along, you!

SHANKSPEARE. Meeee muuuu mooooo mrrrrrr....! *(EXITS)*

STRANGER. What fools these morons be! *(EXITS)*

PIGSTY. We will probably never know what actually happened during those seven problematic years in Shankspeare's life.

PIGSKIN. But we do know that in 1594 the name of Shankspeare appears among the actors performing at the Glob Playhouse in Loin-don.

PIGSTY. The Glob was run by the famous actor Boarbage and we believe that it was Boarbage who suggested and encouraged Shankspeare to move toward a new career.

(BOARBAGE and SHANKSPEARE ENTER.)

BOARBAGE. You're a rotten actor, Shankspeare. I don't say this to encourage you to be better or to challenge you to prove me wrong. I say it because you're just lousy on stage. I've seen sides of beef hanging in the market that have more acting talent than you. And you don't have the looks for it either. You're not the ugliest performer I've ever seen. Swill Kemp is uglier. But he at least is funny. You can't tell a joke on stage to save your life. You're a total washout as a performer and I mean that in the kindest way.

SHANKSPEARE. Thanks for your...er...honesty.

BOARBAGE. You're welcome.

SHANKSPEARE. But what am I to do? The theatre is my life!

BOARBAGE. As well it should be, dear Shankspeare. But the best thing you can do for the Loin-don theatre is to keep off the stage as often as possible.

SHANKSPEARE. But maybe I will get better.

BOARBAGE. When pigs fly.

SHANKSPEARE. I think I will go and kill myself!

BOARBAGE. That's what I like about you, Shankspeare! Always a flair for the dramatic. I knew it the first time you auditioned.

SHANKSPEARE. But you just said—

BOARBAGE. Hold on a second here…*(Pulls a paper from his pocket.)* I found this in your dressing room. *(Reads)* "My Lady Pig's eyes are nothing like the sun…coral is far more red than her mighty snout." Would you care to explain yourself?

SHANKSPEARE. It's just a poem I was working on.

BOARBAGE. A poem! Why do you waste your time on a poem?

SHANKSPEARE. Well, since my acting roles have gotten smaller and smaller lately, I've had a lot of time offstage so I just sort of doodled—

BOARBAGE. Doodled! You shouldn't be doodling with poems. Plays, my dear friend! You should be writing plays! With this flair for the poetic and your natural bent for the dramatic, you could really bring home the bacon!

SHANKSPEARE. Really?

BOARBAGE. Trust me. The theatre needs great playwrights! Look at some of the slop we have to serve our audiences! If the scripts get any worse I'll have to resort to doing French plays. What do you say?

SHANKSPEARE. I'll do it!

BOARBAGE. That's my Shankspeare! Now get to work. I need a new piece with lots of laughs, a bit of romance, and something to do with a Spanish sword that I picked up cheap at the Army-Navy Store. Be inspired. Use your imagination. Climb the heights. Explore places in the heart and mind that have heretofore not been discovered! *(Starts to EXIT.)* Oh, and I need it in a week. So step on it!

SHANKSPEARE. A week!

(BOARBAGE EXITS and a short stool and a small desk covered with papers are set up in the down right stage corner. They will remain there for much of the rest of the play. SHANKSPEARE goes to the desk, sits, take up a quill pen, and writes furiously.)

PIGSKIN. So Shankspeare put away the greasepaint and took up the pen.

PIGSTY. Day and night the new author worked on a comedy called *Loins Labors Lost,* filling it with young love, comic characters, disguises and masks...

PIGSKIN. And a Spanish sword.

PIGSTY. A week later, Boarbage's company was rehearsing the play on the stage of the Glob Playhouse.

(BOARBAGE ENTERS with a few pig ACTORS, including comedian SWILL KEMP, who wears a large fake mustache and carries an elaborate sword, and his page MOUTH. SHANKSPEARE leaves the desk and joins BOARBAGE to watch the rehearsal.)

KEMP. "I hereupon confess I am in love, sweet youth!"
MOUTH. "In love, master?"
KEMP. "By this sword...*(He pulls out sword, swings it, MOUTH ducks to avoid getting hit.)*...it is base for a soldier to love! So I am in love with a base wench! *(Swings again; MOUTH ducks again.)* If drawing my sword against the humor of affection would deliver me from the reprobate thought of it, I would take Desire prisoner! *(A third swing and a third duck.)* Comfort me, youth. What great men have been in love?"

MOUTH. "Ah…Herporkules!"

KEMP. "Herporkules! *(Another swing.)* A pox on that Greek pork roast! Who else?"

MOUTH. "Sa-hamson did love the beauteous maiden Delilah."

KEMP. "Sa-hamson! *(Another swing.)* Curses and dandruff to that hairless hamhock!" *(The ACTORS continue in dumbshow.)*

BOARBAGE. Capital stuff, Shankspeare! That part of the Spanish count Don Armadillo fits Swill Kemp like a pigskin glove! It needs a little cutting here and there. You know, trim the fat. But I think you've got something here. Of course we won't know for certain until Tuesday when we first perform it before the public.

SHANKSPEARE. Tuesday? But do you think it will be ready by then?

BOARBAGE. It doesn't matter. That's when we open. We're already selling tickets. But don't worry, Shankspeare. It's only a play.

SHANKSPEARE. But what if it fails? What if the critics pan it? I'll be ruined!

BOARBAGE. Don't worry about the critics. Most of the population can't read anyway. All you have to do is please the public. Nothing to it. So relax. Water off a hog's back.

SHANKSPEARE. If you say so.

BOARBAGE. By the by, the Queen will be there on Tuesday. *(EXITS)*

SHANKSPEARE. The Queen!

PIGSKIN. Before Shankspeare knew it, Tuesday came. And so did the Queen.

PIGSTY. Good Queen BLT the First, the reigning monarch of Swinedom, imperial ruler of the greatest kingdom on earth, and patroness of the arts!

(BOARBAGE REENTERS with QUEEN who wears a high collar, a crown, and an enormous dress. The rest of the cast is now on stage and all bow to her. She then sits on a throne as the rest stand or sit on the floor and watch the play.)

KEMP. "Comfort me, youth. What great men have been in love?"

MOUTH. "Ah…Herporkules!"

KEMP. "Herporkules! *(Another swing.)* A pox on that Greek pork roast! *(Laughter from audience.)* Who else?"

MOUTH. "Sa-hamson did love the beauteous maiden Delilah."

KEMP. "Sa-hamson! *(Another swing.)* Curses and dandruff to that hairless hamhock!" *(He swings so hard that he falls on the ground; more laughter and applause.)*

PIGSTY. There was laughter, there were tears, there was excitement…

PIGSKIN. And there was that Spanish sword.

PIGSTY. The audience applauded them all!

PIGSKIN. *Loins' Labors Lost* was a hit!

BOARBAGE. *(Shaking SHANKSPEARE's hand.)* By George, you've done it!

QUEEN. *(Coming over to BOARBAGE.)* Quite amusing, Boarbage. Quite amusing indeed. Particularly the sword.

BOARBAGE. Thank you, Your Majesty. *(Bows)* May I present the young playwright? The honorable Shankspeare. *(SHANKS-PEARE bows.)*

QUEEN. We are pleased, Shankspeare. Yes, we are pleased.

SHANKSPEARE. Thank you, Your Majesty.

QUEEN. But the next time, something with a little blood. Not too much, mind you. But a little blood adds to the excitement, don't you agree? We must now depart. Thank you both for an afternoon's diversion. *(Calls)* My carriage! To the royal trough.

(All EXIT but BOARBAGE and SHANKSPEARE.)

BOARBAGE. Did you hear that, Shankspeare? Get to work! Something with blood! We start rehearsals on Saturday.

SHANKSPEARE. Saturday! But I killed myself coming up with the last play. I can't keep cranking them out so fast!

BOARBAGE. Yes you can. Write a good part for me this time. Perhaps a villain. Yes, I'd like that. A treacherous villain. And don't forget the blood.

SHANKSPEARE. But I haven't a clue of what to write about! You can't get silk from a sow's ear!

BOARBAGE. Steal the story from history. How about a king? A bloody king? That will do the trick. I can play a bloody, treacherous king! Just be sure it's not a relative of the Queen. Enough talking. Get to work!

(BOARBAGE EXITS and SHANKSPEARE goes to the desk and writes furiously.)

PIGSKIN. Taking Boarbage's advice, Shankspeare quickly wrote a play about a villainous hunchback who schemes and murders his way to the throne.

PIGSTY. He called it *The History of King Porkrind the Third.*

PIGSKIN. Boarbage played the evil Porkrind and triumphed in the role.

(BOARBAGE ENTERS, limping and hunched over.)

BOARBAGE. "Now is the winter of our discontent, made glorious by this sun of Pork!"

PIGSTY. The play was filled with treachery, battles, revenge...

PIGSKIN. And blood. Plenty of blood.

BOARBAGE. "And therefore, since I cannot prove a lover, I am determined to go hogwild and prove to be a villain!"

PIGSTY. Porkrind murders his brother...

BOARBAGE. "Farewell, Clarence!" *(Stabs an imaginary person.)*

PIGSKIN. He murders his best friend . . .

BOARBAGE. "Farewell, Buckingham!" *(Stabs an imaginary person.)*

PIGSTY. He even murders his nephews, two young princes, as they slept in the Tower of Loin-don.

BOARBAGE. "Bye bye, boys! *(Stabs twice.)* Talk about pigs in a blanket."

PIGSKIN. But by the end of the play, the evil King Porkrind gets his just desserts. *(Sounds of battle.)*

BOARBAGE. "Take that! *(Swinging his sword in battle.)* And that! *(Drops sword and cannot reach it.)* My sword! I need a sword! A knife! Even a pointed stick! A stick! A stick! My kingdom for a stick!"*(Dies and remains on the floor.)*

PIGSTY. Shankspeare's history play was a big hit and the theatre's most promising playwright was off and running.

PIGSKIN. Over the next few decades there would be thirty-three plays by Shankspeare...

PIGSTY. More histories, comedies, tragedies...

PIGSKIN. And not only plays. Often the writer would return to doodling and write poems.

(A pig PUBLISHER ENTERS with several sheets of parchment and reads the top sheet.)

PUBLISHER. "Shall I compare thee to a swineherd's birthday? Thou art more lovely and more temperate than pork chops in May…"

PIGSTY. Shankspeare started sending the poems to publishers.

PIGSKIN. Dozens of love sonnets…

PUBLISHER. "When in disgrace with fortune and swine-like eyes, I all alone beweep my piglike state…"

PIGSTY. And narrative poems as well…

SHANKSPEARE. *(Reads the title page.) Venus and Pigfoot.*

PUBLISHER. *A Lover's Intestinal Complaint.*

PIGSKIN. All of them were published over the years and were read in the best houses and by the most educated of swine.

PIGSTY. Though they did not pay as well as the plays, the poems made Shankspeare a famous literary figure.

(BOARBAGE finally gets up off the floor and goes to SHANKS-PEARE at his desk.)

BOARBAGE. No no no no no no! A waste of time, Shankspeare! Nothing but highfalutin' drivel! Write for the stage…for the porcine populace!

SHANKSPEARE. But a play is over in a few hours. A published poem lives forever! I will be remembered!

BOARBAGE. Books fall apart! Paper rots! Society favorites go out of fashion faster than last year's swine flu!

SHANKSPEARE. I want to be accepted as a great writer, not just some hack who turns out scripts for hams on stage.

BOARBAGE. Then tell me something, hack. How much did

that endless Venus and Pigfoot poem pay? How much went into your piggy bank from the months you spent and the hogsweat you put into it?

SHANKSPEARE. Well…I…

BOARBAGE. Just what I thought. *(Tosses a bag of coins on the desk.)* Get to work, genius. We go into rehearsal in six days. *(EXITS)*

PIGSKIN. So Shankspeare returned to the theatre…

PIGSTY. And continued to enjoy success as one of the most popular "hacks" on the Loin-don stage.

PIGSKIN. He explored the battle of the sexes in the comedy *The Taming of the Shoat…*

PIGSTY. As the brawling lover Porkchopio and the shrewish Katerina Pigiron matched wits and assaults.

(KATERINA PIGIRON, wearing a bright red dress, runs on followed by PORKCHOPIO, wearing an outrageous fathered hat.)

PORKCHOPIO. "Good morrow, Kate. For that's your name, I hear."

KATERINA. "Well have you heard, but something hard of hearing! *(Hits him on the ears.)* They call me Pigiron that do talk of me."

PORKCHOPIO. "Nay, Kate. You lie. *(Steps hard on her foot; she limps away from him.)* You are called Kate the Cutie. Or Katerina the fairest porker of all Verona. Sometimes even referred to as Miss Piggy! *(She crosses to him to hit him but he trips her and she falls.)* And I am here to tell thee, Kate, that I am moved to woo thee for my wife."

KATERINA. "Moved? *(He puts his hand out to help her rise*

but she pulls him to the ground and sits on him.) You'll not move till I say it is time."

PORKCHOPIO. *(Gasping)* "They told me not that such a porker was as light as a feather!"

KATERINA. "Asses are made to bear, and so are you."

PORKCHOPIO. "No. Miss Piggies are made to bear, and so are you! Upon Sunday is the wedding day."

KATERINA. *(Rises)* "I'll see thee hanged on Sunday first!" *(EXITS)*

PORKCHOPIO. *(Rises)* "Well, I'll be hog-tied! I am the swine born to tame this pigheaded porker! I will bring her from pugilant pigiron to peaceful and pleasant as a suckling pig on Mother's Day!" *(EXITS)*

PIGSTY. The variety and vitality of the characters that Shankspeare created were astonishing to behold.

PIGSKIN. From kings and soldiers to peasants and clowns, the plays were filled with memorable pigs of all kinds.

PIGSTY. Sometimes the characters were not limited to the animal kingdom but also included spirits and fairies...

PIGSKIN. As in the magical moonlit comedy *A Midsummer Night's Pig Roast...*

PIGSTY. In which Porkeron, the king of the fairies, plays a trick on Canadian Bacon, the queen of the fairies.

(PORKERON, with a flowing cape, and CANADIAN BACON, wearing a crown and flowing fabrics, ENTER from opposite sides of the stage.)

PORKERON. "Ill met by moonlight, proud Canadian Bacon."

CANADIAN BACON. "What ho, jealous Porkeron! I have forsworn your pigpen and company."

PORKERON. "Return to me the precious little warthog that thou hast stolen!"

CANADIAN BACON. "Not for all the ham in fairyland. I depart and will chide no more with thee!" *(Crosses upstage and goes to sleep on the ground.)*

PIGSKIN. To get even with the proud queen, Porkeron takes a magic flower that, when its liquid is placed on the eyes of someone asleep, that someone will fall instantly in love with the first creature that it sees upon waking.

(PORKERON tiptoes to the sleeping BACON, pours liquid on her eyes, then EXITS. PICKLED-PIG'S FEET, also called PUKE, ENTERS.)

PIGSTY. Also in the forest was the mischievous spirit Pickled-Pig's Feet.

PIGSKIN. But everyone called him Puke for short.

PIG'S FEET. "Over hill, over dale! From pigsty to barnyard pond, I am the most mischievous piggy of them all! *(Noise offstage.)* What's this? A stranger! In our forest? How curious."

(PIG'S FEET hides as the pig workman HOGWILD, wearing work clothes and a hardhat, ENTERS. PORKERON watches as well.)

HOGWILD. "Where be my fellow actors from the Razorback Union? We were to meet in this wood and rehearse the play that is to be performed before the Duke of Squealford. *(Calls out.)* Fellow swine! Where art thou? It is I, Hogwild the union foreman! Where be these fellows?" *(EXITS opposite side of the stage.)*

PIG'S FEET. "I cannot help myself. I will play mischief on this rude mechanical. With my humble magic powers, I will transform him into something quite disgusting. Let me think…Ah! I have it! *(Points off to where HOGWILD exited, casting a spell.)* "By moonlight's mystical myopia, let this muddled moron become that most misshapen of morsels — a mortal!" *(Laughs)* He he he he he he!! Now let his friends get a look at him!"

(HOGWILD REENTERS, but without his pig nose. Note: this is the only time in the whole play in which an actor does not wear a pig nose.)

HOGWILD. "Halloo there! Peter Curlytail! Pigsnout! Snugsnort! Where are you?"

(The pig workman PETER CURLYTAIL ENTERS.)

PETER. "Where are these actors? We are meant to rehearse–" *(Sees HOGWILD and freezes.)*
HOGWILD. "Ah, good Peter Curlytail! Well met, I am sure."
PETER. "O monstrous creature! Come not near me!!" *(Runs off.)*
HOGWILD. "What's the meaning of that?"

(PETER CURLYTAIL REENTERS cautiously.)

PETER. "You…you…you…!"
HOGWILD. "Why do you tremble, Peter Curlytail? Speak your mind."
PETER. "You…you are transformed! Bless me, dear Hogwild, but you have been turned into a…a bacon-eating, sausage-slurping…human!" *(Run off.)*
HOGWILD. "I did not come here to be insulted! Human,

indeed! I never did call him such a name. *(Shouts)* Come back here, Peter Curlytail, and apologize!!"

CANADIAN BACON. *(Slowly awakes.)* "What melodious sounds are these? *(Sits up and sees HOGWILD.)* And what beauteous creature is this?"

HOGWILD. "Oh. I didn't see you there, madam. Do you know the way out of these woods?"

CANADIAN BACON. "I know not one bush or bramble, any stream or stile, dearest and bravest one. All I know is that I love thee as the stars love their heavenly sisters!"

HOGWILD. "All I want is a one-way ticket out of here. So cut the nonsense and point me in the right direction!"

CANADIAN BACON. "Thou art as wise as thou art beautiful! *(Embraces HOGWILD.)* Out of this wood do not desire to go. Thou shalt remain here, for I doth love thee and will have my fairies attend on thee forever after!"

HOGWILD. *(Breaks away from her.)* "A looney porkloin, if I ever saw one! Get away from me! I shall go mad ere I escape from thee!!" *(Runs off.)*

CANADIAN BACON. "Tarry, sweet creature! Tarry until I can win thy heart, you manly mortal of a man!!" *(Rushes off after him.)*

SHANKSPEARE. *(Still at desk.)* What am I doing? Have I gone too far, letting a pretty pig like that fall in love with a human? *(Writes furiously.)*

PIGSKIN. But by the end of the play the spell over the fairy queen is broken and all ends happily.

PIGSTY. A man may make a pig of himself but no one would be satisfied with a pig making a man of himself.

(PORKERON and PIG'S FEET EXIT as SHANKSPEARE leaves the desk and meets with the noble pig SIR FRANKFURT BACON on the other side of the stage.)

PIGSKIN. Soon after *A Midsummer Night's Pig Roast* opened, Shankspeare received a very special visitor.

PIGSTY. It was the distinguished scholar, scientist and nobleman, Sir Frankfurt Bacon.

SHANKSPEARE. This is indeed a great honor, Sir Frankfurt!

FRANKFURT. I had to seek you out, Shankspeare, and let us, as they say, chew the fat together. After I read these poems of yours, I knew I must try my best to persuade you.

SHANKSPEARE. Persuade me to what, Sir Frankfurt?

FRANKFURT. To stop wasting your time with these vulgar plays and concentrate all your energies on poetry.

SHANKSPEARE. But the plays pay the rent and my tailor bills and my health insurance—

FRANKFURT. Four hundred years from now, do you think anyone will care about your tailor and his bills? No. It is the poetry that will live on and enlighten the world!

SHANKSPEARE. I was kinda hoping a few of the plays might stick around as well...

FRANKFURT. Pig droppings! No one cares about plays! They aren't even published. Do you think they will outlast your lifetime? Nonsense. Write for the future, Shankspeare! Look to the ages yet to come...not at ramshackle playhouses that will someday be dust. *(EXITS)*

PIGSTY. Shankspeare was more confused than ever.

PIGSKIN. Should it be plays or poems?

SHANKSPEARE. I must continue to do both. The plays will feed my stomach and the poems will feed my soul. Oh, what a rogue and peasant pig am I! *(Returns to the desk and writes.)*

PIGSTY. So Shankspeare continued to do both.

PIGSKIN. More sonnets and more plays came from the pen of the literary genius.

PIGSTY. Such as the Roman history play, *Julius Razorback...*

(JULIUS and BRUTE CHOPS, both in togas, ENTER.)

PIGSKIN. The story of the emperor Julius Razorback who was betrayed by his best friend, Brute Chops.

BRUTE CHOPS. *(Pulls out a knife.)* "Liberty! Freedom! *(Stabs JULIUS.)* Tyranny is dead!" *(JULIUS falls to the ground.)*

JULIUS. "Et tu, Brute Chops?" *(Dies; both actors freeze in position.)*

PIGSKIN. And there was the Scottish history play, *MacBoar...*

(MACBOAR and LADY MACBOAR, wearing plaid, ENTER.)

PIGSTY. The story of the noble thane MacBoar who is driven to murder the king because his ambitious wife, Lady MacBoar, rode piggy back on him.

MACBOAR. "He's here in double trust; first, as I am his kinsman and his subject, then as his host."

LADY MACBOAR. "Screw your courage to the suckling pig and we will not fail!"

MACBOAR. "Out, out, brief candle. Life's but a walking shadow, a poor player that—"

LADY MACBOAR. "Enough poetry. Kill the king before he dies of old age!"

(MACBOAR raises the knife then both freeze in position.)

PIGSKIN. Then there was perhaps the greatest work of them all...

PIGSTY. *The Tragedy of Hamhock, Prince of Denmark.*

(The pig courtier BALONEYUS ENTERS with QUEEN BURP-TRUDE. A puny curtain on a rod is set up.)

PIGSKIN. The ageless story of a prince gone mad out of love, revenge, indecision...and other things.

BURPTRUDE. "Dear counselor Baloneyus, have you seen my son Hamhock?"

BALONEYUS. "Queen Burptrude, he is coming straight herc to your bedchamber. I will hide myself behind the arras here so that I can hear all." *(Hides behind the curtain.)*

(HAMHOCK ENTERS, all in black.)

HAMHOCK. "Mother!"

BURPTRUDE. "Hamhock, thou hast thy father much offended."

HAMHOCK. "Mother, you have my father much offended!"

BURPTRUDE. "Come, come, you answer with an idle tongue."

HAMHOCK. "Go, go, you question with a wicked tongue." *(Sticks out his tongue at her.)*

BURPTRUDE. "What! Thou wilt not murder me! Help!"

BALONEYUS. *(Behind curtain.)* "Help! Help!"

HAMHOCK. "How now! *(Pulls out a knife.)* A rat or a pig? Dead, for a ducat, dead!" *(Stabs BALONEYUS through the curtain; he falls to the ground.)*

BALONEYUS. "O, I am one slain swine!"

BURPTRUDE. "O me, what hast thou done?"

HAMHOCK. "Is it the king?" *(Looks at the body.)*

BURPTRUDE. "O, what a rash and bloody deed is this!"

HAMHOCK. "Baloneyus! Thou wretched, rash and intruding fool, farewell!" *(All three freeze in position.)*

PIGSTY. All in all, Shankspeare murdered some fifty-seven characters between 1596 and 1606.

PIGSKIN. A record not broken until the invention of video games some four hundred years later.

(JULIUS, BRUTE, MACBOAR, LADY MACBOAR, HAMHOCK, BURPTRUDE and BALONEYUS all EXIT. SHANKSPEARE puts down his pen and slumps over the desk wearily.)

PIGSKIN. But Shankspeare was getting older...

PIGSTY. And richer...

SHANKSPEARE. I don't know how long I can keep doing this. Oh, I am aweary of this theatrical life! Why don't I retire? I have enough money. I could move to the West Indies...or even Florida.

PIGSTY. But it was easier said than done. For once a pig has tasted the power of creation, it is hard to go back to the pig sty.

SHANKSPEARE. So back to work. *(Picks up quill pen.)* This time...a great love story. *(Writes)* "The Tragedy of Swineo and Drooliet...Two pigpens, both alike in dignity, in fair Verona we lay our scene..."

(The pig lovers SWINEO and DROOLIET ENTER. DROOLIET stands on a bench to represent a balcony.)

DROOLIET. "O Swineo, Swineo! Wherefore art thou, Swineo? Deny thy papa pig and refuse thy name!"

SWINEO. *(Approaching her.)* "Call me but love and henceforth I never will be Swineo again!"

DROOLIET. "What hog art thou that so stumblest on my soliloquy?"

SWINEO. "By a name I know not how to tell thee who I am. Call me porkpie, call me Porky Pig, call me Wilbur, call me Oscar Mayer! What's in a name? Hog swill by any other name would smell as sweet!"

DROOLIET. "It is Swineo! It is my love!"

(The entire company, including the QUEEN, ENTERS and sits or stands to watch the last scene of the play. SHANKSPEARE joins them. DROOLIET lies on the bench as if dead and SWINEO pulls out a small bottle of poison.)

PIGSTY. The Glob Theatre was packed for the opening night of Swineo and Drooliet.

PIGSKIN. Everyone who was anyone was there, including Good Queen BLT the First.

SWINEO. "Ah, dear Drooliet, why art thou yet so fair? Dead but still the beauteous pig of my heart. I will stay with thee, and never from this palace of dim night depart again. *(Holds up the poison.)* Come, bitter conduct! Come poisonous guide! Here's to my love! *(Drinks, coughs, collapses.)* Oh, all-knowing Walgreen's…thy drugs are quick. Thus with a kiss I die."

*(He kisses DROOLIET then falls to the floor. After a second.
    DROOLIET awakes.)*

DROOLIET. "Where is my lord? I do remember well where I should be. But where is my Swineo? *(Sees the body.)* What! Dead? *(Picks up bottle and smells.)* Poison, I see, hath been his timeless end. So too will I drink! *(Drinks but it is empty.)* What? No friendly drop to help me die? *(Shouts heard offstage.)* Someone is coming! There is no time! My true love's dagger! *(Takes dagger from SWINEO's body.)* Then I'll be brief. O happy dagger...*(Stabs herself.)* Now I am but pork on a fork..."

(She dies dramatically then BOARBAGE ENTERS and addresses the audience.)

BOARBAGE. A gloomy morning at the pigpen place...the sun for sorrow will not show its face...for never was a story of more woe....than this of Drooliet and her Swineo.

(Applause from the spectators. QUEEN BLT rises from her throne and crosses over to SHANKSPEARE.)

QUEEN. We believe you have quite surpassed yourself, Shankspeare.

SHANKSPEARE. Thank you, Your Majesty.

QUEEN. Yes, quite entertaining. You managed both romance and blood. I quite like that. We think you are something of a wizard, Shankspeare.

SHANKSPEARE. A wizard, Your Highness?

QUEEN. You create characters and then determine their destiny. That is a very powerful gift. I pray you do not abuse it.

SHANKSPEARE. No, Your Majesty.

QUEEN. My carriage! Now to the royal trough. *(Starts to go but stops.)* Oh, another thing, Shankspeare.

SHANKSPEARE. Yes…?

QUEEN. Stick to the plays. Those poems of yours do put us to sleep every time. Concentrate on the theatre.

(All EXIT but SHANKSPEARE.)

SHANKSPEARE. I fear my time as a playwright and a poet is soon to end, dear queen. A wizard, she says. But even a wizard must eventually tire of magical powers. And I am indeed tired. This next play will be my last. I will use it to say farewell to the theatre and to Loin-don and…everything. But what story this time? What ideas have I not already exhausted? Come on, wizard, think of something—That's it! A play about a wizard! *(Goes to desk and writes.)*

PIGSKIN. And so Shankspeare sat down and began his last play...*The Pork Test.*

PIGSTY. The main character was the wizard Porcino who has magical powers and controls the weather, all the animals, and even the spirits of the air.

(PORCINO, wearing a flowing cape, ENTERS with a long staff. Lightning and thunder, then he addresses the heavens.)

PORCINO. "Ye elves of hills, brooks, standing lakes, and groves…thou mutinous winds from the green seas and the azure skies…Ye creatures of two and four and who-knows-how-many legs…All hear me, Porcino, your master and keeper!" *(More thunder and lightning.)*

PIGSKIN. By the end of the play, Porcino forgives his enemies, gives his beloved daughter to the hog who loves her, and decides to give up his magical powers and return to the farm.

PORCINO. "But this rough magic I here abjure…and even now will break my staff and bury it certain fathoms deep in the earth. *(Breaks the staff in two.)* And as for my book of potions and spells, I'll drown it deep in the ocean!" *(More thunder and lightning, then PORCINO exits.)*

PIGSTY. And that is exactly what Shankspeare did.

PIGSKIN. Shankspeare left Loin-don and returned to the small town of Fatsford-on-Avon, the place of his birth.

(SHANKSPEARE rises from the desk and crosses to the center of the stage.)

SHANKSPEARE. Good old Fatsford. I never knew how much I missed it until now.

PIGSTY. But Shankspeare did not return to the humble pigpen of the past.

PIGSKIN. With money in the pocket, Shankspeare was able to buy the best barn in town and lived out the final years in simple but comfortable luxury.

SHANKSPEARE. We are such stuff as dreams are made on, and our little life is rounded with a sleep. Here in Fatsford will I retire and my every third thought shall be of my grave. *(Exits)*

PIGSTY. And so Shankspeare remained in Fatsford until the day the great author quietly and peacefully died.

PIGSKIN. Goodnight, sweet Shankspeare. May flights of angels sing these to thy rest.

PIGSTY. The roast is silence.

(The desk and stool are removed. The entire company returns as TOURISTS, half of them joining PIGSKIN on one side of the stage while the other half joins PIGSTY on the other side.)

PIGSKIN. This way, ladies and gentlemen!

TOURISTS. Oink! Oink! Oink! Oink! Oink!

PIGSTY. Follow me, please!

TOURISTS. Snort! Snort! Snort! Snort! Snort!

PIGSKIN. We are now inside one of the most hallowed of places in Fatsford-on-Avon. It is in this church that Shankspeare is buried.

PIGSTY. This section of Westhamster Abbey is known as the Poets' Corner and to my right you can see the monument to Shankspeare.

TOURISTS. Snort! Snort! Snort! Snort! Snort!

PIGSKIN. You can see the tombstone just to the left of me here.

TOURISTS. Oink! Oink! Oink! Oink! Oink! *(They take pictures.)*

PIGSTY. A few years after Shankspeare was buried in Fatsford-on-Avon, a good number of the plays were actually published in a large book called the Fat Folio. Soon Shankspeare was recognized as the greatest dramatist of all Swinedom.

PIGSKIN. You can barely make out the epitaph on Shankspeare's grave, it is so worn after all these years. But I will read it to you. It says: Fellow swine, behold my fate And do not fear to celebrate. Blest be those who pop their cork And curst be he that moves this pork.

PIGSTY. Now everyone back in the bus. Next stop: the Tower of Loin-don.

TOURISTS. *(As they EXIT.)* Snort! Snort! Snort! Snort! Snort!

PIGSKIN. We have one more stop on our tour and that's Anne Hogaway's Cottage. This way please…

TOURISTS. *(As they EXIT.)* Oink! Oink! Oink! Oink! Oink!

*(All are gone [Including PIGSKIN and PIGSTY] except SHANKS-
PEARE who stands alone upstage.)*

SHANKSPEARE. Our revels now are ended. These our
piglike actors were all spirits and are melted into air, into thin air.
(Moves down toward the audience.) And like the baseless fabric of
this swinish vision, all the mighty towers, gorgeous palaces,
solemn temples, even this very theatre and all who are in it — all
shall dissolve and, just as this insubstantial pageant faded, leave no
trace behind. But for now, let your applause resound throughout
this space and its noise will echo through the ages. *(With a Porgy
Pig stutter.)* Tha-! Tha-! Tha-! That's all folks! *(Bows)*

END OF PLAY

PROPERTIES AND COSTUME PIECES LIST

Plastic pig noses on elastic strings (entire cast)
Cameras and camcorders (tourists)
Wooden sword (Actor 1)
Helmet and sword (Shankspeare)
Sailor hat (Shankspeare)
Long hooded cloaks (Shankspeare, Spy and Stranger)
Letter (Spy)
Poem on parchment paper (Boarbage)
Desk, stool, quill pen, parchment papers (Shankspeare)
Fancy sword (Swill Kemp)
Crown (Queen BLT)
Wooden sword (Boarbage)
Sheets of parchment (Publisher)
Bag of coins (Boarbage)
Crowns (Porkeron and Canadian Bacon)
Flower (Porkeron)
Hardhat (Hogwild)
Daggers (Brute Chops, MacBoar, Hamhock, Swineo)
Free-standing curtain on rod (Baloneyus)
Bench to stand on and then lie on (Drooliet)
Bottle of poison (Swineo)
Cape and long staff (Porcino)

www.ingramcontent.com/pod-product-compliance
Lightning Source LLC
Chambersburg PA
CBHW071931130726
47909CB00014B/2978